The Kids in Mrs. Z's Class

Poppy Song Bakes a Way

The Kids in Mrs. Z's Class

Poppy Song Bakes a Way

KARINA YAN GLASER

illustrated by **KAT FAJARDO**

Series coordinated by Kate Messner

ALGONQUIN YOUNG READERS
WORKMAN PUBLISHING
NEW YORK

Copyright © 2024 by Karina Yan Glaser
Illustrations copyright © 2024 by Kat Fajardo
Cover art color and interior shading by Pablo A. Castro
Kraft paper texture © klyaksun/Shutterstock

Algonquin Young Readers
Workman Publishing
Hachette Book Group, Inc.
1290 Avenue of the Americas
New York, NY 10104
workman.com

Algonquin Young Readers is an imprint of Workman Publishing, a division of Hachette Book Group, Inc. The Workman name and logo are registered trademarks of Hachette Book Group, Inc.

Design by Neil Swaab

Library of Congress Cataloging-in-Publication Data is available.
ISBN 978-1-5235-2652-9 (hardcover)
ISBN 978-1-5235-2653-6 (paperback)

First Edition October 2024 LSC-C
Printed in Indiana, USA, on responsibly sourced paper.

10 9 8 7 6 5 4 3 2 1

For beloved grandmothers everywhere,
especially my own Po Po,
and my children's grandmothers,
Gramma and K-Mum

MEET
The Kids in Mrs. Z's Class

Adam

Ayana

Carlota

Emma

Chapter 1
The Best Lunch Box

It was almost lunchtime, and Poppy Song could not wait. Lunch was her favorite part of the day, because her lunch box always had something special in it.

It was the same lunch box that her grandma, whom Poppy called Po Po, had used when she was a little girl living in Hong Kong. There were many dents in it, but that didn't bother Poppy. Papa always said that each dent told a story. The lunch box had three small round trays stacked on top of one another, held together with metal clasps. Her grandmother always tucked something special into each one.

The bell finally rang. Poppy tapped the tips of her toes on the floor under her chair as she waited for Mrs. Z to dismiss each table to go to the lunchroom. When Mrs. Z finally called her table, Poppy fast-walked to the shelf where they kept their lunches.

As she reached for her lunch box, she saw Memo was there, even though his table was called second. He used crutches because he fell out of a tree in August. The crutches slowed him down.

"I can carry your lunch," Poppy offered. "If you want."

Memo looked at Poppy, and Poppy wondered what he thought about her. She had tried to make her pigtail buns extra neat this morning. And she was wearing her favorite overalls, the blue ones with a red heart on the right pocket. Po Po had embroidered that heart so Poppy would remember that Po Po loved her all the time, even when they weren't together.

"Sure, thanks, Poppy," Memo finally said, and Poppy glowed. It was the first time he had said her name, and wasn't it so nice when someone said your name for the first time?

They headed to the lunchroom together. Because of his leg, Memo had an elevator pass. Theo usually accompanied Memo on the elevator, but Theo had been called to the office right before lunch and hadn't returned. Poppy held her lunch box in one hand and Memo's lunch bag in her other hand. Poppy thought she should make conversation, but she didn't know what to say.

"You like baking, right?" Memo said, breaking their silence. "I watch *The Great British Baking Show* sometimes."

Poppy smiled, relieved. Baking was something she could talk about! "I want to be on that show one day. My grandma, Po Po, is the best baker in the world, and she's teaching me everything she knows. She's going to be the Valued Visitor next Tuesday."

"Lucky!" Memo said. "I can't wait for my turn. Rohan's mom was so cool."

Poppy nodded. "It's even more exciting because next Tuesday is Po Po's birthday! I want to bake her something really special as a surprise."

"Ooh, yes," Memo said. "What's your favorite thing to make?"

"Po Po and I make a lot of Chinese desserts,"

Poppy said. "My favorite is cream buns, but we also make almond cookies, sponge cakes, egg tarts, Dragon's Beard candy—"

"Wait a second," Memo said, his eyes lighting up. "Dragon's Beard candy sounds like the best dessert ever!"

"I've only made it with Po Po," Poppy admitted. "She says it's called that because it looks like the beard of a dragon. It's really hard to make!"

When they got to Memo's table, she put his lunch down next to Theo. Wyatt was sitting on Theo's other side.

"Hi, Poppy!" the boys at the table said.

"For the next Valued Visitor Day, Poppy's grandma is coming! And Poppy is going to make Dragon's Beard candy!" Memo said.

"I don't know if I'm *definitely* making that—"

Poppy said, but the boys didn't hear her.

"That sounds amazing!" Theo said. "Perfect for dragons like us!"

Poppy wasn't sure what to think about them being dragons. But she was new to Peppermint Falls, so she pretended to understand what they were talking about. "It's made from spun sugar," she explained.

"I love sugar!" Theo said.

"Want to sit with us?" Memo asked.

"I promised Olive I would sit with her," Poppy said. "But thank you."

Poppy said goodbye, then made her way to her usual table. It was true that Dragon's Beard candy was super hard to make, but it *was* a good idea for Po Po's birthday. The last time they made it together, a year ago, Po Po had told her it had been her favorite treat when she was growing up.

But could she make the candy by herself and keep it a surprise from Po Po? Poppy wasn't so sure.

Chapter 2
Dragon's Beard Candy

Poppy glanced at everyone's lunches as she walked through the cafeteria. Some kids purchased lunch at school, and today it looked like pasta and green beans. Other kids had brought lunch from home. Fia had a container of what looked like rice and curry. Ruthie had something that looked really fancy: spring rolls with a small cup of red sauce on the side. Lucy had a huge bag filled with pretzels.

Today, Rohan, Olive, and Sebastian were

together at their regular table, and Synclaire had joined them. She was wearing a shirt that said *I ♥ NYC*. Sebastian was peering down at a thick book about whales.

"There you are!" Olive said, her fabric lunch bag unopened on the table in front of her. She was finger knitting with sparkly purple yarn. By the time Poppy sat down, Olive had ended the knit rope she was making and tied the ends together. Then she slipped the knitted necklace over Poppy's head.

"Voilà!" Olive said. "That's a fancy French way of saying 'Here you go!' We were waiting for you before we started to eat. Well, except for Rohan." She glared at him.

Rohan froze, his sandwich already half gone. "Sorry! I couldn't wait," he said, his mouth full. "My stomach was telling me it needed something in it, fast!"

Poppy laughed as she opened her lunch box and spread her three food trays on the table.

"Ooh," Synclaire said, looking over. "What's in your lunch today?"

"My grandma and I made mini pineapple buns yesterday. She put a bunch in my lunch box to share with you," Poppy said. "Do you want some?"

Of course everyone wanted one. Olive made grabby hands as Poppy passed a tray around.

"These buns are delicious," Olive said to Poppy.

Sebastian touched a napkin to the side of his mouth. "Please tell your grandmother she is a superb baker."

"You can tell her yourself!" Poppy said. "She's coming to school next week for Valued Visitor Day!"

"Hooray!" said Rohan. "My mom loved being the Valued Visitor."

"Will she bring more of these pineapple buns?" Olive asked.

"Actually," Poppy said, "on the day she comes, it will be her birthday! So I thought *I* should make something for *her*!"

"Ooh, what are you going to make?" Synclaire asked.

Poppy thought about her conversation with Memo. Po Po had been teaching Poppy so much about baking. If Poppy could make Dragon's Beard candy all by herself, then Po Po would know she had taught Poppy well. It would be the best birthday present.

"Dragon's Beard candy," Poppy said with conviction. "It's made from very thin strands of sugar, sort of like cotton candy."

Olive, Rohan, Sebastian, and Synclaire

cheered. Emma, who was sitting at the table next to theirs, asked, "Why's everyone so happy?"

Olive gave her an update, and word spread throughout the lunchroom within minutes. By the time they got in line to return to their classroom, *everyone* in Mrs. Z's class knew about the Dragon's Beard candy. And everyone was excited!

Chapter 3
Starting Over

The rest of the day went by quickly. When the bell rang, Poppy collected her lunch box and backpack and headed out the door to the school bus. She didn't live very far from Curiosity Academy, but her parents didn't trust her to walk to and from school by herself yet, even though plenty of kids in her class did it every day. Thunder was even allowed to ride her bike to school, and she lived a mile away!

Poppy walked to the front of the school with Rohan, Fia, Sebastian, and Wyatt, where the yellow school bus was waiting for them. They climbed aboard, and Poppy took a seat in the front with Wyatt, who had the longest bus ride home out of all of her classmates. He showed her his watch. It had a stopwatch in it! He started the timer as the bus rumbled to life, and three minutes and twenty-three seconds later, Poppy got off at the first stop. She walked down the steps of the bus to find her very favorite person in the whole world sitting on the bench in front of Crunch Time Fitness. Po Po!

Her grandmother broke into a big smile when Poppy ran into her arms.

"How was your day?" Po Po asked, hugging Poppy tight.

"Exciting!" Poppy said, and she told Po Po

about how happy everyone was about Po Po coming to their school for Valued Visitor Day. They climbed the stairs to their apartment on the second floor. While Po Po unlocked the door, Poppy looked toward the third floor, where their neighbor Ms. Kellogg lived. They had become really good friends with Ms. Kellogg because Po Po shared lots of treats with her.

Some kids in her class didn't know what they wanted to be when they grew up, but Poppy had it all figured out. She wanted to be a baker, just like Po Po.

Before the Songs moved to Peppermint Falls, Po Po had her own Chinese bakcry in New Jersey. Happy Valley Bakery had been Poppy's favorite place in the whole world. When she was little, she would go to the bakery and Po Po would give her lumps of dough to play with. Then, when Poppy was four years old, Po Po taught her how to make almond cookies. When Poppy had taken her first bite of the first cookie that she and Po Po baked together, Poppy knew she wanted to be a baker. She imagined them working side by side in the bakery when Poppy was older.

But then Po Po retired, and Papa's best friend from college mentioned they were hiring a receptionist at the dental practice he worked at. Papa took the job, and the whole family moved to Peppermint Falls.

Peppermint Falls was nice, but it was very different from where the Songs used to live. It didn't have Poppy's old house with the cozy nook in her bedroom where she could snuggle into blankets and read books. It didn't have a deck where her family would eat dinner and watch the sunset turn the sky blue and purple and orange. It didn't have her best friends who she had known since preschool.

Now, every night when they ate dinner, they could hear loud pop music from the evening cardio class at Crunch Time Fitness downstairs. Sometimes, if the class required a lot of jumping, the building would tremble to the beat. Poppy's bedroom was small, just big enough for a bed and a beanbag chair. There was no view of the sunset from any of their apartment windows.

Moving to Peppermint Falls had meant starting over, learning a new neighborhood and school, and making new friends. Po Po made friends easily because she always shared her baked goods with everyone, like Ms. Kellogg.

Even though Poppy was friendly with people at Curiosity Academy, she thought that bringing in Dragon's Beard candy for her whole class would guarantee that everyone would like her.

Then, maybe, Peppermint Falls would feel more like home.

Once inside the apartment, Poppy went to the refrigerator and took out the little container where she kept chopped vegetables and fruits for her parakeets, Dumpling and Wonton. She said hi to the birds, fed them their afternoon snacks, then left the door to their cage open so they could fly around before dinner.

"We will make tang yuan for snack, yes?" Po Po asked.

"Okay!" Poppy said. She loved tang yuan, which was a sweet dumpling of rice flour filled with roasted black sesame seeds. Po Po liked to make the dumplings with a little beetroot juice, which turned them pink.

While Po Po took a jar of black sesame seeds from the cupboard above the stove, Poppy grabbed a mixing bowl from a lower cabinet by the sink and set it on the counter. But when Poppy turned around, Po Po was standing by the open pantry, staring inside but not moving.

"Po Po?" Poppy asked. She had never seen Po Po not in motion in the kitchen.

Po Po seemed to wake up. She shook her head. "I forgot what I was looking for. I don't remember where anything is in this new kitchen!"

Poppy smiled and reached past Po Po to take down the container of rice flour.

"That's what I needed," Po Po said. "Thank you, Poppy."

Together they toasted sesame seeds, then made a dough from rice flour, beetroot juice, and hot water. Po Po was so good at baking that she didn't even need to measure anything! After shaping the dough into balls and filling them with sesame seeds, they boiled the tang yuan in a ginger-sugar syrup. A minute later, the dumplings were ready. Po Po spooned them into two small bowls with just enough of the ginger-sugar water to cover them, keeping them warm and soft.

Po Po glanced at the kitchen clock. "Calvin should be home soon if you want to eat with him."

"Okay," Poppy said, wrapping her arms around Po Po and breathing in her

grandmother's comforting scent. This was the best type of afternoon, making delicious desserts and spending time with her favorite person in the whole world.

Chapter 4
Kitchen Mix-up

Ten seconds later they heard the lock turn. Calvin, Poppy's older brother, appeared. He was still wearing his shin guards from after-school soccer practice. His eyes lit up when he saw the tang yuan.

"Yum!" Calvin said. Po Po hugged him even though he looked really sweaty and had bits of grass all over him.

"Aren't you having any?" Poppy asked Po

Po, looking at the two dishes on the round kitchen table.

"I'm not very hungry," Po Po said. "I had a big lunch."

After Calvin washed his hands, they sat at the table while Po Po did the dishes and put the ingredients away. Poppy inhaled the steam from the dumplings, but it smelled a little off to her—more like the briny ocean than a sweet dessert.

Calvin scooped one dumpling up in his spoon and slurped it. Then he coughed and spit the tang yuan back into his spoon.

Poppy raised her eyebrows at him, and he just shook his head slightly. She carefully put the spoon to her mouth and bit into the dumpling. It was so salty! But there was no salt in the recipe . . . unless Po Po accidentally used salt instead of sugar for the ginger syrup!

Po Po hummed as she cleaned, her back toward them, and Calvin gestured for Poppy to give him her bowl. She slid it over, and Calvin took both bowls to the bathroom and got rid of the contents. He returned to the kitchen and put one of the empty bowls back in front of Poppy.

"Thanks so much!" Calvin told Po Po as he washed his bowl in the sink and set it on the drying rack. "I'm going to take a shower." He gave her a kiss on the cheek.

Poppy slowly walked to the sink and washed her bowl, too. She looked at Po Po out of the corner of her eyes. Po Po was cleaning the counter with a wet towel and seemed totally normal, but Poppy was uneasy.

She had never known Po Po to mess up a dessert before, ever.

"Ready for a recipe?" Mama asked that night after Poppy had finished practicing the piano, brushed her teeth, and climbed into bed.

"Yes!"

Mama picked up a rectangular wooden box from Poppy's bookshelf. Inside were dozens of Po Po's recipes, all written in her grandmother's careful handwriting.

"Anything you want in particular?" Mama asked.

"Can you read Dragon's Beard candy?" Poppy asked. "I'm going to surprise Po Po by making it for her birthday."

Mama's eyebrows raised. "That's a difficult recipe."

"I know," Poppy said. "But it's one of Po Po's favorite treats. I want to make her something she really loves."

"After I married your dad," Mama said, "Po Po tried to teach me how to make it. It was a disaster, and I ended up covered in strands of sticky sugar. It was in my hair, up my nose, everywhere!"

Poppy giggled, imagining Mama wrapped up in a candy web, unable to escape.

"Po Po was so happy when you liked baking so much," Mama continued. "Now she has someone to pass her recipes on to."

Mama found the Dragon's Beard candy recipe and began reading. There were a lot of steps. First, you had to boil sugar, corn syrup, a tiny bit of vinegar, and water to a certain

temperature. Then you had to pour it into doughnut molds. When it was cool enough to handle, you removed it from the molds. Then came the messy part.

To make the delicate strands of candy, you had to pull the molded sugar circle until it was twice its size, twist it into a figure eight, fold it into two sets of circles, and dip it into a cornstarch-and-rice-flour mixture to keep the circles from sticking together. Then you pulled, twisted, folded, and dipped it again and again. If you did it right, the sugar turned into little strands, like cotton candy. Po Po's recipe said to pull and fold it eight times total, which would make 2,048 strands by the end!

When Mama finished reading, she put the card back into the box. "That sounds like a big project," she said to Poppy.

Poppy nodded. It was worth going through

all the trouble if it meant that Po Po would be surprised. Mama tucked the covers around Poppy so she felt as snug as a hot dog in a bun, and Poppy fell asleep thinking about dragons with fluffy white beards.

Chapter 5

Brown Bag Lunch

Poppy was thinking about Po Po and the salty tang yuan the next morning when she put on her third-favorite overalls, which were light pink. As she pulled the left strap over her shoulder and slid the buckle over the button to secure it, she noticed that Po Po had stitched a small red heart on this pair, too. It was on the front chest pocket, right over where Poppy's own heart was. Poppy smiled.

She left her bedroom and found Mama in the kitchen putting a box of cereal and a carton of milk on the kitchen table.

"Where's Po Po?" Poppy asked. Ever since Po Po retired, she had been making breakfast for Poppy and Calvin.

"She's sleeping in today," Mama replied.

Poppy frowned. Her grandmother was always the first person awake. "Is she okay?"

Mama nodded. "She's just feeling tired this morning."

Calvin came out of his room and wrinkled his nose when he saw the cereal and milk. "I just woke up from a dream where Po Po made congee and crullers. I was hoping I dreamed it into reality."

"Maybe I should try making congee one day," Mama mused.

Calvin and Poppy exchanged a glance. Mama was great at lots of things. She could knit comfy sweaters and take group photos where no one was blinking or making a weird face. She regularly ran half-marathons. But she was terrible, just *terrible*, in the kitchen.

"Poppy, I was thinking about you making Dragon's Beard candy," Mama said, "and I wondered if you wanted to ask Ms. Kellogg if you could use her kitchen. That way you can keep it a surprise for Po Po."

"That's a good idea!" Poppy said.

Poppy used Mama's phone, and Ms. Kellogg said Poppy could come over the next day after school. Poppy gave Mama a list of ingredients she needed, and Mama said she would drop them off at Ms. Kellogg's place later.

After Poppy finished her breakfast, Mama handed her a brown paper bag.

"Lunch for you!" Mama said. "Hurry, the bus will be here in three minutes."

Poppy took the bag. "Where's my lunch box?"

"I thought you might want a brown bag lunch for once, instead of carrying that heavy lunch box," Mama said.

Poppy shoved the lunch bag into her backpack and followed Calvin down the stairs and onto the street. When the bus screeched to a stop in front of them, Poppy and Calvin got on.

The first thing Wyatt said when Poppy took the empty seat next to him was, "You forgot your lunch box!"

Poppy shook her head. "My mom made my lunch today. I put it in my backpack."

"Cool," Wyatt said, patting his own

backpack. "The candy you're making sounds amazing!"

Poppy nodded, but she didn't say anything else. She kept thinking about Po Po. A few minutes later, the bus dropped them off in front of the school. Without her lunch box, Poppy felt like she was missing something really important.

"Good morning!" Mrs. Z called as Poppy and her classmates filed into the classroom. "Take a seat at your desk and start the Daily Scribble."

Poppy put away her things and sat down. Around her was lots of noise. Lucy was already asking Mrs. Z if she could go to the nurse. Carlota and Fia were comparing their new bracelets. Olive was sitting at the desk across from Poppy, picking at the pink eraser at the top of her pencil.

The Daily Scribble
for wednesday, october 2

If you could invent a new dessert, what would it be?

If this was yesterday's Daily Scribble, Poppy would have lots of ideas, like fruity cream puffs or nian gao cupcakes. Sometimes she would have an idea for a new dessert, and she and Po Po would try making it. But today she was not in the mood for invention, so she wrote:

My grandma is the best at making desserts. My grandma already makes all of my favorites. I don't want her desserts to ever change.

Poppy knew she didn't really answer the question, but she did not want to think about change today.

When the egg timer went off, Mrs. Z called on a few people to share.

Memo's favorite dessert was coffee ice cream, and he wanted cotton candy that tasted like coffee.

Sebastian wanted to create a mango rice pudding.

Mars wanted green tea–flavored doughnuts to be a thing.

"I can't wait until Poppy's grandma comes next week," Olive announced. "Poppy is making Dragon's Beard candy so we can celebrate her grandma's birthday!"

Poppy looked down at her notebook and pushed the tip of her pencil down into the lower left corner of the page, so hard that it left a dark mark and dented a lot of the pages underneath it. She really hoped she could make that candy. Everyone was counting on her.

It was time to put away their writing notebooks and get ready for math. The morning felt very long, and Poppy couldn't even look forward to lunch.

When her table was called to go down to the cafeteria, Poppy grabbed her brown-bag lunch and peeked inside.

Instead of a steamed bun filled with roasted pork or a raisin twist bun or an egg custard tart, her lunch bag held a sunflower-butter-and-jelly sandwich, a granola bar, an apple, and a bag of crackers. And the granola bar was the dry oatmeal kind, and the

only person in her family who liked those was Calvin.

Poppy swallowed her disappointment.

Chapter 6
A Little Tired

After a long day at school, Poppy got on the school bus. As it headed toward Main Street, Poppy remembered that Po Po had slept in that morning. She was suddenly struck with a fear that Po Po wouldn't be waiting for her. What would she do then? Would the bus driver let her off without an adult to pick her up? She didn't have a key to the apartment.

Thankfully, when the bus pulled up to the curb in front of her building, Po Po was sitting on the bench, just like always. Poppy got off the bus and wrapped her arms around her grandmother.

"Are you feeling better?" Poppy asked, absorbing Po Po's comforting warmth.

"I'm a little tired," Po Po admitted. "I'm sorry I didn't make your lunch today. Was it okay?"

"It was fine," Poppy said. She didn't want Po Po to feel bad.

"I have something for you," Po Po said, taking something from her pocket.

It was a sticker of a smiling cupcake for Poppy's sticker collection!

"I love it!" Poppy said. "Thank you!"

They went up the stairs to their apartment, Po Po moving slower than usual. Poppy put her bag down by the front door.

"How about I get us snacks today?" Poppy

said to Po Po. "We could watch *The Great British Baking Show*." It was their favorite program. They had watched every season and always tried to predict who would win. Sometimes Poppy liked to imagine putting on an apron and being in the baking show tent, making something so beautiful and delicious that the judges would declare her the winner.

Po Po nodded and headed to the living room, where she slowly lowered herself onto the couch. Poppy put the cupcake sticker in her sticker book, then went to the kitchen and rummaged through the cupboards. Po Po had baked every day since they arrived in Peppermint Falls, so they hadn't kept a lot of other snacks around. Poppy finally found an old bag of trail mix that Papa had bought over the summer. She brought it over to the couch where Po Po was looking around her, confused.

"Have you seen the remote?" Po Po asked.

Poppy set the bag of trail mix on the coffee table and looked in the usual places: on the console in front of the television, inside the side table drawers, and in between the sofa cushions. No remote.

Po Po wrung her hands. "I just saw it this morning. I watched the news. I had it in my hands."

"It's okay," Poppy said. "I'm sure Calvin can find it when he gets home from soccer practice. He's so good at finding everything."

But Calvin wouldn't be home for another two hours, so their television show would have to wait. Poppy might as well start her music homework.

"Do you want to practice the recorder with me?" Poppy asked Po Po.

"Yes!" Po Po said, her mood instantly brightening.

Poppy went to the bookcase where Papa had bought two more recorders once he saw that Poppy was learning how to play at school. Papa had loved playing the recorder when he was in third grade.

Calvin was not a fan of the instrument. Mama didn't like it, either. She made a rule that Poppy, Po Po, and Papa could only practice when she and Calvin were out of the apartment.

Poppy's class had already learned "Hot Cross Buns" and "Mary Had a Little Lamb." Mrs. Berry had said they were improving quickly. Poppy suspected it was because

Mrs. Berry gave out candy if the whole class practiced.

"Mrs. Berry taught us 'Old MacDonald Had a Farm' today, and it's so hard," Poppy said. "She told us it was fourth-grade recorder material."

"That sounds difficult," Po Po said. "We should probably practice a lot."

Poppy showed Po Po how to play the song. "Old MacDonald Had a Farm" was tricky because there was a whole section with the same note over and over again, and it had to be played in the correct rhythm. When they tried it, Poppy and Po Po did not play it in the same rhythm at all! Sometimes Poppy played it too fast, and Po Po played it too slow. Then Po Po tried to speed up, and Poppy played even faster and then started moving her feet like she was dancing an Irish jig. Then Po Po imitated her, and they both collapsed on the couch, laughing. It is impossible to play the recorder while laughing.

The phone rang, and Poppy ran to pick it up. It was Ms. Kellogg, their upstairs neighbor.

"Hi, Poppy," Ms. Kellogg said. "I was wondering if you could be done with recorder practice for the day? I'm working on a new painting, and the, uh, music is interrupting my flow."

"I'm sorry, Ms. Kellogg," Poppy said, making a face at Po Po that said, *Oops, we're in big trouble!* Po Po made a face back at Poppy that said, *Oh no! Sorry!* "We're done practicing now," Poppy told Ms. Kellogg.

Ms. Kellogg's voice had a note of relief in it. "Thank you, Poppy. And I look forward to seeing you tomorrow for you-know-what."

Ms. Kellogg was referring to Dragon's Beard candy practice, of course.

"Me too," said Poppy. "See you then!"

After Poppy hung up, she looked at Po Po. "Ms. Kellogg would like us to stop."

"Too bad," Po Po said.

Poppy put her recorder inside the used sock that Mrs. Berry had given to all the third graders for their instruments. Po Po's recorder had a real case with a snap closure, because Papa had bought hers from Lintowongan, the music store in town. While Po Po put her recorder away, Poppy went into the kitchen to get a glass of water. Practice made her thirsty.

She opened up the freezer to get ice cubes.

Next to the ice cube tray, she found the television remote.

Chapter 7
Pizza Night

Po Po was so relieved when Poppy showed her the remote. She even laughed. Then they watched an episode of *The Great British Baking Show*. While Po Po made her usual comments to the bakers ("Whip the egg whites more!" or "*Fold* the flour in, gently, gently!"), Poppy got lost in her thoughts.

She was thinking about Po Po, and not just the events of the last couple of days. There had been other little things. A set of clean mixing bowls appeared in the refrigerator, and a couple of cans of coconut milk were in the cupboard where the water glasses usually were. Po Po hadn't been eating as much, and she seemed more tired than usual.

That evening, after Calvin came home from soccer practice, Poppy went into his bedroom. He was sitting at his desk doing homework. She used the tip of her toe to nudge his gross soccer clothes to the side, made her way to his bed, and sat down. Dumpling the parakeet followed her and perched on her shoulder. Poppy fished out some sunflower seeds from the front pocket of her overalls, where Po Po had embroidered the heart, and fed them to him.

Calvin spun in his desk chair to face her. He had a mini basketball in his hand, and

he aimed it at a toy hoop that hung over his closet door. He missed. "What's up?"

Poppy picked at a piece of lint on his comforter. "Are you worried about Po Po?"

Calvin's eyebrows raised. Without standing up, he rolled himself closer to Poppy and she handed him a sunflower seed. He fed it to Dumpling. "Are you talking about yesterday?"

Poppy nodded. "And other things."

"I mean, the salty tang yuan was weird, but I don't think it's a big deal," Calvin said. "I've mixed up ingredients before. Remember?"

Poppy smiled at the memory. Calvin had switched salt and sugar when making a Mother's Day cake for Mama a few years ago. Papa had to throw it out. Calvin was so upset that he cried.

"She put the remote control in the freezer

today," Poppy said. "And doesn't she seem more tired?"

"I haven't noticed her being more tired," Calvin said. "She seems pretty normal to me."

"Hmm," Poppy said.

Then Calvin rolled himself back to his desk and dropped his forehead on top of his open math textbook. "I've got so much homework this year. You're lucky you're only in third grade."

Poppy left Calvin alone with his math and went back into the living room. She filled up the seed tray in her parakeets' cage. Dumpling flew right in, and Wonton, who had been dozing off on a little perch by the bookshelf in the living room, awoke at the sound of the seeds and followed Dumpling inside.

Poppy closed the cage door just as the front door opened. Papa came in along with the wonderful smell of pizza.

Calvin was out of his bedroom in point-five seconds. "Are we having pizza?"

"Yes, we are!" Papa said, setting the box on the dinner table.

Po Po eyed the pizza with suspicion. "I was just about to make dinner."

"You deserve a break," Papa said, giving her a side hug. "Picking up dinner is the *yeast* I could do."

"Papa!" groaned Calvin and Poppy at the same time. Mama just laughed. Po Po shook her head, but smiled.

Papa looked at Mama and kissed her on the cheek. "I a-*dough* you."

"Please stop," Calvin said, covering his eyes.

"Hey," Papa said. "You don't *pepper-own me!*"

Poppy grinned. "You're so *cheesy*."

"That's what I'm talking about," Papa said, holding his hand up to Poppy for a high five.

While they ate, Poppy wondered whether she should tell her parents about what happened with the tang yuan yesterday or the remote today. Poppy looked at Po Po, who was eating a slice of pizza and laughing at something Mama had said. Nothing seemed wrong, so Poppy tried to put the idea out of her head.

There was no need to worry anyone by bringing it up.

Chapter 8

Nowhere in Sight

On Thursday, everything seemed to go back to normal.

Po Po was making breakfast when Poppy came out of her room in the morning. Poppy's metal lunch box was packed and ready to go, and when Poppy opened it at lunchtime, she found mini egg tarts inside, which she shared with everyone at her table. The egg tarts were a hit. Sebastian told her it was the dessert he did not even know he needed.

After school, Poppy went home on the bus to find Po Po waiting for her.

"You're going to Ms. Kellogg's place today, right?" Po Po asked as they went up the stairs.

Poppy nodded.

"I'm in the middle of making red bean buns," Po Po said. "They should be done by the time you get home."

"Yay!" Poppy said. She loved red bean buns, and she could bring any extras to school the next day.

After dropping off her book bag, Poppy went upstairs and knocked on the door.

"Hi, Poppy!" Ms. Kellogg said.

Poppy stepped into the apartment. By the window, there was a canvas on an easel on top of a drop cloth. It was a painting of a leopard, but instead of yellow fur and black spots, Ms. Kellogg used only shades of purple in her painting.

"I love that," Poppy said. "My friend Rohan is an artist. He draws animals, too."

"Invite him over one day, and we can paint animals together," Ms. Kellogg said, leading Poppy to the kitchen, where the ingredients they needed were on the counter. "So, you're going to show me how to make Dragon's Beard candy?"

Mama had made a copy of the recipe, and Poppy pulled it from her pocket.

"I'll need your help with the stove," Poppy said. "My mom says I'm not allowed to turn the burner on or use the oven without an adult until I'm in middle school."

Ms. Kellogg nodded. "That sounds smart."

Poppy measured out the ingredients into a large pot on the stove. Then she clipped a candy thermometer to the side, and Ms. Kellogg turned the stove on low. Poppy watched the thermometer carefully.

Once the mixture had reached the right temperature, Ms. Kellogg turned off the flame. She poured the sugar mixture into the doughnut molds while Poppy helped keep it neat using a spatula. While they waited for the liquid to cool, Poppy measured rice flour and cornstarch into a bowl to use when they pulled the candy.

When she finished, the sugar mixture was still too hot to handle, so Poppy told Ms. Kellogg she was going downstairs to grab her math book so she could do homework.

When Poppy opened the door to her apartment, however, the oven timer was going off. A burning smell filled the air.

"Po Po?" Poppy called out.

She ran through the apartment. She didn't see Po Po in the kitchen, or in the living room, or in her bedroom.

Poppy looked at the oven. She was not

allowed to touch the oven without supervision, ever. Should she call 9-1-1? There wasn't a fire . . . yet. But what if the buns caught on fire inside the oven?

Poppy left her apartment, dashed up the stairs, and burst back into Ms. Kellogg's place.

Ms. Kellogg saw the look on Poppy's face and said, "What's wrong?"

"Can you help me turn off the oven? My grandmother left, and I can't find her—"

"Of course," Ms. Kellogg said immediately, following Poppy down the stairs.

The oven timer was still beeping. Ms. Kellogg grabbed oven mitts and opened the oven door. Smoke poured into the kitchen as she pulled out the tray of burnt red bean buns.

Ms. Kellogg turned off the oven and opened the windows.

Now that there was no more risk of fire, Poppy felt cold all over. Where was Po Po?

Ms. Kellogg gave her a hug. "Let me call your parents, then we'll go look for your grandma, okay?"

Poppy nodded. A minute later, they went downstairs. Poppy scanned Main Street.

Po Po was nowhere in sight..

Chapter 9
I Am Lost

Poppy did not know what to do. Everything felt very scary.

Ms. Kellogg kneeled down in front of Poppy. "Your parents are coming. We can look for your grandma, or we can go back up to your apartment. What do you want to do?"

Poppy brushed a hand across her eyes. "Can we look for her?"

"Of course," Ms. Kellogg said. "Let's bring

a photo with us so we can show people what she looks like."

They ran back upstairs, and Poppy grabbed her favorite framed photo of her and Po Po in front of the old bakery. Then she took Ms. Kellogg's outstretched hand and they headed down the stairs to the street.

They went into Crunch Time Fitness, but no one there had seen Po Po. They went into the library, the post office, and the Makery, which was a crafts shop. They showed people Po Po's photo in each place. When they still hadn't found her, Poppy spotted the sign on the next door: Sweet Bun Bakery.

She knew before she had even opened the door that her grandmother was there.

Bursting into the bakery, she found Po Po sitting at a table. An employee with a plastic

tag with the name *Jasper* on it was sitting next to her.

"Po Po!" Poppy cried, running toward her.

Po Po smiled at the sight of Poppy and pulled her into a hug.

"I am lost," Po Po said simply.

"It's okay," Poppy said. "I found you."

Behind her, Poppy heard Jasper talking to Ms. Kellogg, saying that Po Po had seemed very confused and kept asking why the menu had changed so much. A second later, Papa came into the bakery, relief filling his face when he saw Po Po and Poppy.

After thanking Jasper for his help, Poppy, Po Po, Papa, and Ms. Kellogg headed back to their building. Mama and Calvin were waiting in their apartment.

"Thank goodness," Mama said, getting up

from the dining room table and giving Po Po a hug. "Are you hungry? Tired? Do you want to lie down for a little bit?"

Po Po said she was tired, and Mama led her to her room. A few minutes later, Mama shut the door and joined Poppy, Calvin, and Papa at the round kitchen table. Poppy explained what had happened.

"You did a great job, Poppy," Mama said when Poppy finished. "You did the exact right thing going to Ms. Kellogg."

"Were you scared?" Calvin asked. "I would have been scared."

Poppy nodded, then turned to her parents. "Po Po has been really forgetful lately. She's been losing things and putting stuff in weird places."

"A couple of days ago, she switched sugar

and salt when she made tang yuan," Calvin added.

"We should have told you before, but we didn't think it was a big deal," Poppy said.

Mama and Papa glanced at each other.

"Po Po has been struggling with her memory for the last six months now," Papa said. "That's part of the reason why we helped her close the bakery."

"I thought it was because the landlord raised the rent so high she couldn't afford it anymore," Calvin said.

"That, too, but she was also having trouble," Mama told them. "We thought she just needed more rest. But I think the move and the change in her routine have gotten her feeling even more confused. Today shows it might be more serious than we've thought."

"I'm going to call the doctor and set up

an appointment," Papa said, pulling out his phone. He left the table and drifted into the living room to make the call.

"Is Po Po going to be okay?" Poppy asked Mama, biting her thumbnail. "She's supposed to be my Valued Visitor at school on Tuesday. All my friends want to meet her. I'm making Dragon's Beard candy for her birthday!"

Mama shook her head. "I don't know, Poppy. Let's see if she can see the doctor before then."

"Maybe we shouldn't have moved to Peppermint Falls," Poppy said, sniffling.

There was a long pause, and then Calvin said, "I sort of like it here. My soccer team is really great."

Poppy didn't want to admit it, but she liked Peppermint Falls, too. She liked Curiosity Academy and Mrs. Z and her classmates and the pizza parlor. She was even getting used to the loud music from Crunch Time Fitness. But was it worth leaving their old home if it was bad for Po Po?

Chapter 10
Little Kindnesses

The next day at school, the morning began with Emma talking about which special day it was.

"Today is," Emma said, pausing for dramatic effect, "National Cinnamon Bun Day!"

Carlota raised her hand. "I love cinnamon buns."

Theo raised his hand. "Me too."

"Me too!" Synclaire yelled.

Mrs. Z raised her eyebrows. "If you like

cinnamon buns, raise your hand."

Everyone but Sebastian and Ayana raised their hands.

"How can you not like cinnamon buns?" Emma asked the anti-cinnamon-bunners.

"They have extra things on them," Sebastian explained. "Like nuts."

"I hate raisins," Ayana said with a shrug.

Olive raised her hand. When Mrs. Z called on her, she said, "Poppy's grandma always puts extra treats in Poppy's lunch box to share with our table. She made cinnamon buns a couple of weeks ago, and they were delicious!"

"Can I sit at your table today?" Fia asked Poppy.

"Me too?" Mars said.

"I want to sit with you!" Adam and Carlota said at the same time.

"But if you all sit with Poppy, then there won't be room for me or Sebastian or Olive!" Rohan exclaimed.

Poppy's stomach started to hurt. Po Po had a doctor's appointment today, and if Po Po was sick, maybe she wouldn't be able to bake anymore. Then Poppy's lunches wouldn't have special things in them, and her class-mates wouldn't want to sit with her anymore. And maybe Po Po would forget more and more things. Maybe one day she wouldn't remember Poppy anymore!

Poppy knew she had to master the Dragon's Beard candy. She needed Po Po to know how much Poppy loved her.

She raised her hand. "Can I go to the nurse?"

A few minutes later, Poppy stood in the doorway of the nurse's office. Her classmate

Lucy was already there. Lucy was always in the nurse's office. Ms. Reyes was on the phone, but she gestured for Poppy to come inside and take a seat.

"Are you feeling okay?" Poppy asked Lucy as she sat down.

Lucy shrugged. "Are *you* feeling okay?" she asked Poppy.

"My stomach hurts," Poppy said.

Lucy nodded knowingly, then reached underneath her seat and pulled out what looked like a small beanbag wrapped in plastic. She took the plastic off, twisted the bag, and shook it a few times.

"Here," Lucy said, handing it to Poppy. "It's a hand warmer, but I put this on my stomach when it hurts. Sometimes it helps."

Poppy took the bag. It felt good, like holding a warm cup of tea. She put it against her stomach. It *did* make her feel better.

"Thanks, Lucy," Poppy said.

"No problem," Lucy said.

Ten minutes later, after Ms. Reyes examined her and determined that Poppy was okay, Poppy headed back to her classroom and watched the clock. A few days ago, lunch was her favorite time of day. Now, she dreaded it, especially because her mom had packed her lunch again.

Also, everyone wanted to sit with her because they thought she had extra desserts.

Also, maybe Po Po wouldn't come to Valued Visitor Day, and Poppy would have to explain why.

When the bell rang for lunch, Poppy dragged her feet as she collected her lunch bag. Memo was also moving slowly, until they were the last two people in the room. When he saw her brown lunch bag, he asked, "Where's your lunch box?"

Poppy shook her head. "At home." Then she looked at Memo. She knew he had a grandmother because she had seen him with her after school.

"My grandma isn't doing well," Poppy said. Then she burst into tears.

Poppy was so embarrassed. Memo was probably wishing he got out of the classroom faster. She guessed he would flee to the lunch-room. But a moment later, she heard a crinkling sound, and Memo put something into her hand. Poppy used her other hand to swipe at her tears. When her vision cleared, she saw what Memo had given to her.

Inside a clear plastic container was a piece of cake.

"It's tres leches cake," Memo explained. "My grandmother made it for my mom's birthday yesterday. There were leftovers."

"You should have it," Poppy said, sniffling. "I don't want to take your dessert."

"We can share," Memo suggested.

Poppy looked at the door, then back at Memo. "I don't really want to go to the lunch-room. Everyone expects me to have extra dessert, and I don't want to explain why my grandma didn't pack my lunch today."

Mrs. Z came back into the classroom and smiled with relief at the sight of Poppy and Memo.

"Ah," she said. "I wondered where you two were!"

Memo spoke up before Poppy could say anything. "Can we eat lunch in here?" He pointed to his leg. "I don't feel like going all the way to the cafeteria today."

"Of course you can stay here," Mrs. Z said. "Are you feeling okay?"

Memo nodded. "It's just one of those days, you know?"

Mrs. Z put an arm around his shoulder. "I know all about those kinds of days."

Poppy looked at Mrs. Z and Memo in surprise. She couldn't imagine that Mrs. Z, who was always cheerful and wearing fun jewelry, could ever have a bad day. And there was Memo, who never seemed bothered by much, but he must also understand bad days. He did have a cast on his leg, after all.

Poppy guessed bad days and hard things happened to everyone. She sat down, and Memo handed her an extra spoon as he opened the container. They both took a bite of cake.

Then they said, "This is sooooo good!" at the exact same time, which made them laugh.

She was grateful for Memo, and for Mrs. Z, and for tres leches cake, and for Lucy and the hand warmer. Little kindnesses added up, and soon, with her stomach and heart full, she felt ready for the rest of the school day.

Chapter 11
The Lunch Box Returns

On Sunday, with just two days left until Valued
Visitor Day, Poppy still had not mastered
Dragon's Beard candy. Back on Thursday,
the day her grandmother had gotten lost, she
had forgotten all about the candy-in-progress.
On Friday, she went to Ms. Kellogg's place
to find that the sugar had turned as hard as a
rock in the doughnut molds. She would have
to start over.

On Saturday, they made the sugar syrup
again and poured it into the molds, which had

six compartments. After it had cooled enough, Poppy and Ms. Kellogg each removed a piece from one of the molds, pulled it apart, and twisted it into a figure eight, just like Po Po's recipe said. They folded the figure eight in half, dipped the circles into the rice flour and cornstarch mixture, and pulled and twisted it again. Then the strands broke in Ms. Kellogg's hands, and the candy fell into the tray, causing the flour mixture to erupt in a little cloud around them.

"You're so good at that, Poppy," Ms. Kellogg said as she watched Poppy twist and pull the strands.

"Oh no," Poppy said. "I've lost count of how many pulls I've done. I think I did too many." Her candy strands had gotten so thin that they had melted back into one another in a clump.

They tried again, but this time Poppy pulled too fast and the candy broke. Ms. Kellogg pulled too slowly, and the strands hardened and cracked.

"This is really difficult," Ms. Kellogg said, their failed attempts lying on the counter. "I don't know how your grandma does this!"

They each had one more try, but when they went to remove the last pieces from the molds, it was too late. The sugar had cooled and hardened too much to pull. Poppy started to cry.

"Maybe we should take a break," Ms. Kellogg said, putting an arm around Poppy. "Let's try again tomorrow."

The next day, Poppy got ready to go back to Ms. Kellogg's place again. Papa and Po Po had gone on a walk, and Mama was doing laundry. Calvin watched Poppy put the ingredients into a bag as he munched on an apple in the kitchen.

"Where are you going?" he asked.

"Upstairs to try to make Dragon's Beard candy again," Poppy said. "I keep messing up, and it has to be perfect for Po Po's birthday."

"Why does it have to be perfect?" Calvin asked.

"So she knows how much I love her!" Poppy said. "And she might forget that soon."

Calvin took another bite of his apple. After he had chewed and swallowed, he said, "Po Po wouldn't want you to be so worried about the candy. She just wants to spend time with you. She knows how much you love her already. How could she not?"

Poppy considered Calvin's point. Po Po delighted in being in the kitchen with Poppy, because they were doing something they enjoyed, together.

"I'm right, right?" Calvin said.

"You are right," Poppy admitted.

Calvin aimed his apple core at the trash can. The core flew through the air, hit the rim, and bounced on the floor.

"Ew," Poppy said. "You have the worst aim."

Calvin shrugged. "I can't be the best at everything."

On Monday morning, Poppy woke up and found Po Po in the kitchen making breakfast.

"Po Po," Poppy said. "Do you think we could bake something together after school?"

x

"Of course," Po Po said. "That is my favorite thing to do."

Mama joined them. "Can I help? I know I'm not a baker, but I'm a good cleaner!"

At the doctor's recommendation, Mama had talked to her boss and changed her schedule for the week so she would be home in the afternoons when Poppy came home from school.

Po Po pulled Mama and Poppy into a hug. "I would love that. Let's make cream buns. Poppy's favorite."

At eight forty-five on the dot, Mrs. Z got everyone's attention. Emma announced that it was National Play Outside Day. Mrs. Z showed everyone her earrings, which were little dangling astronauts. Then she reminded everyone that tomorrow was Valued Visitor Day.

"Poppy, is there anything you would like to share about your valued visitor?" Mrs. Z asked.

Poppy nodded. She took a deep breath. At the table next to her, Memo gave her a thumbs-up. Poppy looked around, knowing she was going to disappoint everyone with her news. She fidgeted with the bottom of her shirt sleeve, then said, "I've been looking forward to having my grandmother come for Valued Visitor Day."

It looked like Olive was about to say something, so Poppy hurried on. She didn't want to start her speech all over. "You all know my grandma is the best baker. She used to own her own bakery when we lived in New Jersey, before we moved here. But lately she's been really forgetful, so my parents took her to the doctor. The doctor did some tests, and she says my grandma might have Alzheimer's."

"What is that?" Steven asked. "Al-something?"

"Alzheimer's," Poppy said. "It's a disease that makes my grandma mix up things or forget what she's doing."

Carlota raised her hand. "My friend's grandpa has Alzheimer's," she said. "He confuses my friend with someone else in the family."

Poppy paused, thinking about how that might feel with Po Po. "Anyway," she continued, swallowing, "I'm not sure if Po Po will come tomorrow. It depends on how she's feeling. It might be hard because she's never been here before, and that might make her more mixed up than usual." She took a deep breath. "Also, I tried making Dragon's Beard candy, and it was too hard for me to make by myself. The candy strands would break every time I tried pulling them. So I'm not bringing any tomorrow. I'm sorry."

There was a long silence, and Poppy could feel the disappointment in the room. Disappointment that she wouldn't be bringing in Dragon's Beard candy the next day. Disappointment that Valued Visitor Day was ruined. Would anyone want to be her friend after this? Poppy looked down at her hands.

"Wyatt, do you have something to say?" Mrs. Z asked.

Poppy looked up in surprise. She had never seen Wyatt raise his hand before.

"I see your grandma wait for you at the bus stop every afternoon," Wyatt said. "She's always there, even when we had that big rainstorm two weeks ago. She must love you a lot."

"She's my favorite person in the whole world," Poppy whispered.

"My grandma is a little scary," Memo admitted. "I wish we got along like you and your grandma."

"I'm sorry your grandma isn't feeling well," Synclaire said. "And it's okay that you're not going to bring in Dragon's Beard candy. It sounds really hard to make."

"I know you'll be able to do it one day," Olive said. "Because you're a good baker."

And all around her, the students in Mrs. Z's class nodded their heads in agreement.

"You really think so?" Poppy said.

"Really!" said a whole lot of voices at once. When Poppy looked around, she saw her classmates looking back at her, smiling.

They didn't look disappointed.

They didn't look mad.

They looked understanding.

"How about we start our Daily Scribble?" Mrs. Z said, clapping her hands. Her astronaut earrings jiggled as if they were dancing. She went to the board and wrote:

The Daily Scribble
for Monday, October 7

Who is someone important in your life?

Poppy knew just how to answer that question.

Chapter 12
Valued Visitor Day

Poppy woke up with a start on Tuesday morning. Her thoughts felt scrambled, as if there was something important happening that day. And then it all washed over her. There were *two* important things happening today.

It was Po Po's birthday, and it was Valued Visitor Day.

She propped herself up in bed and peeked out the window. Dark clouds were a blanket across the sky, raindrops falling steadily. Of all the types of weather out there, this was her least favorite.

Poppy opened a dresser drawer and looked inside for something to wear. She chose a red-and-white-striped shirt and her number-one favorite pair of overalls. As she pulled on her shirt, her finger touched something that felt different from the soft cotton. When she looked closer, she saw a tiny embroidered heart on the hem. She smiled.

Poppy put on her overalls, then she grabbed purple socks. And there, on the toe of one of the socks, was another little heart.

Poppy ran out of her bedroom. Papa was at the stove, scrambling eggs. Mama was clearing the dishwasher. Calvin was putting his soccer uniform in his backpack.

And Po Po was sitting at the table with a cup of tea.

Poppy ran straight toward Po Po and put her arms around her. "Did you stitch all of these new hearts on my clothes?" she whispered into Po Po's ear.

Po Po turned her head and kissed Poppy's cheek. "It's a reminder that I'm always with you. Do you understand?"

And Poppy understood, really understood, what Po Po had been trying to do with the hearts. It wasn't just to remind Poppy of Po Po when they were in different places. It was a reminder that even if times got hard, or Po Po's memory faded, nothing could take away the moments they had shared.

"Hurry up and eat," Mama said to Poppy. "It's time to go to school."

Poppy looked at Mama.

Mama smiled, already knowing what Poppy was thinking about. "Po Po is having a good day and wants to go to Valued Visitor Day. But I thought Papa and I could tag along, if that's okay? I already asked Mrs. Z."

Poppy couldn't think of a better solution.

After breakfast, they walked to school with umbrellas aloft. Poppy had a small rainbow umbrella, and Po Po had a large rainbow umbrella. When they arrived, Poppy took Po Po's hand and led the way to her classroom. The morning bell had already rung, so there were fewer kids in the hallway than usual. Poppy looked up at Po Po uncertainly, hoping she wasn't feeling too overwhelmed. Po Po just smiled back at her.

They were the last to arrive. Mrs. Z came right over to greet Po Po, Mama, and Papa. She was wearing a sun earring on her left ear and a moon earring on her right. On the board, one of Poppy's classmates had written "Happy Birthday, Poppy's Grandma!"

Poppy and Po Po sat at the front of the class in chairs. Poppy's parents stood in the back, taking photos. Poppy introduced Po Po, and Po Po shared stories about her childhood.

"Hong Kong has wonderful bakeries," Po Po said. "When I was growing up, I walked to school and I would pass by three different bakeries. For my birthday and on special holidays, my mother would let me choose one thing from one bakery. I had to think about my choices very carefully."

Po Po's neighbor taught her how to bake when she was a teenager. She went on to work at her favorite Chinese bakery, one of the ones she had passed by on her way to school, for twenty years. When she moved to America, she opened up Happy Valley Bakery, named after the Hong Kong district she grew up in.

"People came from miles and miles away to buy her pastries," Poppy told everyone. "She's teaching me everything she knows."

"Was she the one who taught you how to make Dragon's Beard candy?" Sebastian asked.

Poppy nodded. "I'm sorry I couldn't bring any today."

Olive spoke up. "Actually, some of us thought that we might bring something to share with you and your grandma, since you two always bring extra things for us in your lunch. My mom and I made carrot muffins." From under her desk, she took out a container filled with muffins in colorful wrappers, plucked one out, wrapped it in a napkin, and gave it to Po Po.

"My grandmother and I made red velvet cupcakes with cream cheese frosting," Synclaire announced to everyone. "When we lived in New York City, there was a bakery around the corner that had the best red velvet cupcakes. Grandma pestered them for the recipe before we moved. But Mrs. Z said I can't give them out until after lunch because it's a lot of sugar." Synclaire looked at Po Po. "But you're an adult, so if you want to eat it now, you can." Synclaire handed her a cupcake.

Memo raised his hand. "My sisters and I made pastelitos. They're filled with guava and cream cheese, and it's one of my favorite desserts." Memo gave Po Po a small container filled with golden triangles of puff pastry. There was another, larger container with more on his desk.

"When I share something I've baked," Po

Po said, her lap now filled with desserts, "it is a way to give you a piece of myself and my culture. Thank you for sharing a piece of yourselves through your food. I feel very loved with these beautiful desserts."

Poppy looked around her, at her classmates who were sharing a piece of their homes with her, and her heart felt warm and full.

Mrs. Z thanked Po Po for coming, and then all of Poppy's classmates wanted to give Po Po a hug. Wyatt gave her two hugs. Then everyone ate the carrot muffins, which were delicious. Mrs. Z said they would save the other treats for after lunch.

A few minutes later, Poppy walked Po Po and her parents out to the hallway so she could say goodbye.

"I love you," Poppy said to Po Po, hugging her tight.

"I love you, too," Po Po said.

When they stepped apart, Po Po tapped a finger on the heart embroidered on Poppy's overalls. "You are always in my heart, no matter what."

Poppy watched Po Po and her parents walk down the hall and disappear around a corner before she stepped back into Mrs. Z's classroom. It was time for the Daily Scribble, and then it would be time for ELA, and then it would be time for math. And after *that*, it would finally be lunch.

Red velvet cupcakes with cream cheese frosting and pastelitos were waiting for her and her friends.

Poppy couldn't wait.

© Corey Hayes

About the Author

KARINA YAN GLASER started writing her first novel when her uncle dared her to write a book. Now she is the *New York Times* bestselling author of the Vanderbeekers of 141st Street series, which has been translated into twelve languages and optioned for film. Her standalone novel *A Duet for Home* earned three starred reviews, was featured on the *Today* show, was selected for numerous best-of lists and nominated for ten state book awards, and was a Teen Readers' Choice Award finalist, among other honors. One of her proudest achievements is raising two kids who can't go anywhere without a book. She lives in New York City with her husband, two teenagers, and an assortment of rescue animals.

Karina's favorite thing about third grade was her teacher, Mrs. Lehner, who read aloud every single day and taught Karina and her classmates how to play "Hot Cross Buns" on the recorder.

karinaglaser.com

About the Illustrator

KAT FAJARDO (they/she) received a Pura Belpré Honor for Illustration for their first graphic novel, *Miss Quinces* (published in Spanish as *Srta. Quinces*). Born and raised in New York City, Kat now lives in Austin, Texas, with their pups, Mac and Roni.

katfajardo.com

The Creators of
The Kids in Mrs. Z's Class

William Alexander

Tracey Baptiste

Martha Brockenbrough

Christine Day

Lamar Giles

Karina Yan Glaser

Mike Jung

Hena Khan

Rajani LaRocca

Kyle Lukoff

Kekla Magoon

Meg Medina

Kate Messner

Olugbemisola Rhuday-Perkovich

Eliot Schrefer

Laurel Snyder

Linda Urban

Read on for a preview of Book Four in the series,

The Legend of Memo Castillo

BY WILLIAM ALEXANDER

Chapter 1

A Game of Sorcery

The legend of Memo Castillo began with a game of cards.

It was Saturday, and almost dinnertime. Memo sat on the floor of his room, broken leg resting on a pillow. His ankle itched under the cast. He tried to ignore the itch. He had more important things to focus on, because Theo had just thrown a lightning bolt at him.

"Zap!" Theo said. "You lose four points."

"Ow," Memo said.

"This game is confusing," Wyatt said.

"You'll get the hang of it," said Memo.

"Watch this. I'm going to attack him with an army of bunnies!"

He played a card with a picture of sword-swinging rabbit warriors on it.

Memo and Theo were teaching Wyatt how to play Sorcery—a game with a bazillion different kinds of collectible cards. Each card was a magic spell like "Throw Lightning Bolt" or "Summon Ferocious Rabbits." Playing the game was like fighting a magical duel.

"Can I cast my own lightning bolt?" Wyatt asked.

"Nope," Theo said. "You do not have enough crystals."

Wyatt frowned at his cards. "This game is *really* confusing."

Memo, Theo, and Wyatt were all classmates at Curiosity Academy. It was a new school this year, so Memo didn't really know most of the other kids. He did know Theo, though. They had been best friends since kindergarten, when they tried to invent time travel with juice boxes.

Wyatt was a new friend. He sometimes sat at the dragon table during school lunch, so Memo had invited him to join their Saturday Sorcery game. Wyatt didn't seem to be having very much fun, though. He put down his cards.

"You two should finish the game without me," Wyatt said. "Can I draw something on your cast?"

"Sure," Memo said.

Wyatt took a marker from his backpack and started to draw a purple dragon on Memo's ankle, which still itched. Memo held his breath and tried to make the itch go away. It didn't work.

"How did you hurt your leg?" Wyatt asked.

"I was reading," Memo said.

"Really?" Wyatt asked. "Was it a dangerous book?"

"He tried to read in a tree," Theo explained. "Then he fell asleep, fell out of the tree, and broke his leg in four places."

"Ouch," Wyatt said while trying not to laugh.

"Maybe the tree was mad about the book?" Theo wondered. "Books are made of paper. Paper is made out of trees. This tree probably rocked him to sleep on purpose. Then it tossed him to the ground."

Memo threw a pillow at Theo and missed.

"It's your turn," Memo said, "and we need to practice for the tournament. Cast your next spell!"

"What tournament?" Wyatt asked.

"The GREAT SORCERY TOURNAMENT at MagiCon," Theo announced.

Wyatt still looked a little bit lost. "Magi-what?"

"It's a big gathering of geeks," Memo explained.

"It is so much more than that!" Theo said. "We went to the MagiCon convention last year, and it was amazing. My dad was one of the volunteers. All sorts of science fiction and fantasy stuff got packed into one building in the city. They had costumes and comics and authors and actors and NASA engineers answering everybody's silly questions."

"And a Sorcery tournament," Memo added, "which Theo and I are *absolutely* going to win this year."

"We'll play as a team," Theo said.

"We'll cast powerful spells," Memo said.

"And we will defeat last year's champion, Josh Harkan," Theo swore.

"Is he that fifth grader who dresses like a vampire?" Wyatt asked.

"That's him," Memo said. "Do you want to come with us?"

"You'll need a costume," Theo pointed out. "I plan to be a cyborg. Half human, half robot."

"I'll be an elf," Memo said.

"Sounds fun," Wyatt said, though he looked like he didn't really want to join a great big gathering of costumed geekery.

"It's still your turn," Memo said to Theo. "Cast your spell, Sorcerer!"

The Kids in Mrs. Z's Class